Thunderbowl

Lesley Choyce

Orca soundings

D0187848

ORCA BOOK PUBLISHERS

Library and Archives Canada Cataloguing in Publication

Choyce, Lesley, 1951-
Thunderbowl / Lesley Choyce.

(Orca soundings)
ISBN 10: 1-55143-552-7 (bound).-- ISBN 10: 1-55143-277-3 (pbk.)
ISBN 13: 978-1-55143-552-7 (bound).--ISBN 13: 1-55143-277-9 (pbk.)

I. Title. II. Series.

PS8555.H668T48 2004   jC813'.54   C2004-900487-5

Summary: Who needs school when you're going to be a rock star?

First published in the United States, 2004
Library of Congress Control Number: 2004100595

Orca Book Publishers gratefully acknowledges the support for its
publishing programs provided by the following agencies: the Government
of Canada through the Book Publishing Industry Development Program
and the Canada Council for the Arts, and the Province of British Columbia
through the BC Arts Council and the Book Publishing Tax Credit.

Cover design: Lynn O'Rourke
Cover image: Getty Images

Orca Book Publishers
PO Box 5626, Stn. B
Victoria, BC Canada
V8R 6S4

Orca Book Publishers
PO Box 468
Custer, WA USA
98240-0468

www.orcabook.com
Printed and bound in Canada.
Printed on 100% PCW recycled paper.
10 09 08 07 • 7 6 5 4

For my daughters,
Sunyata and Pamela
—L.C.

Other titles by Lesley Choyce,
published by Orca Book Publishers

Refuge Cove
(Orca Soundings)

Chapter One

"I'm nervous," Drek complained as we drove toward The Dungeon, a local nightclub famous for its live music. It was going to be our first real public performance. Al was driving the old Dodge van that his grandfather had left him when he died. The floorboards were so rusted out that you could look down and see the road.

"Be cool," Al said as we turned a corner and two mike stands fell over. "Forget there's anybody out there."

"Yeah," I said. "Just pretend we're still back in your basement practicing." We had practiced until we were perfect.

Steve Drekker plays synthesizer and Alistair Cullen is on drums. My name is Jeremy, but Drek and Al call me Germ. I play a mean guitar. I started out playing air guitar in my bedroom. Now it's the real thing. My old man is still kicking himself for buying me the guitar. He saw me in my room one day. I had on the Walkman, cranked wide open. I was jumping up and down whaling on my guitar. The only problem was that I didn't have a guitar. I was just pretending. But I could feel it. It was me playing those riffs. So my father went out and bought me this dumb nylon-string guitar.

I took lessons for three months. The dude who taught me thought I should get into country music. I told him, no way.

So I sold the nylon, sold my bike and a bunch of CDs. With the money I bought an *el cheapo* electric and a crummy little amplifier. It drove my mother nuts. She started going out to the movies with my old man just to get away from the noise. Even my dog stopped hanging out in my bedroom.

And then one day I saw this ad posted in the music store. "WANTED: Lead guitar for new band. Must have experience and be into alternative music." Hell, I had experience coming out of my ears. I'd been listening to music for years. And I was into any kind of music they wanted me for.

Fortunately for me, Thunderbowl wasn't into rap or country or oldies. I knew just about every song they threw at me. And suddenly I was one of them. What I didn't know was that the band was going to get me into so much trouble.

There are only three of us but once we crank up the amps and start rocking, you'd think we were an army. Drek has all sorts of tricks with the keyboard. He has patches and loops and an orchestra packed up in there and a jungle full of animal noises. If you want to hear what it sounds like to be taking off on the space shuttle, just ask Drek to play it back on a digital loop at full volume.

Drek is a tall, nervous guy who wears glasses. He's probably an electronics genius, but he'd rather drink beer and get into fights. Figure that one out.

Alistair Cullen is shorter than I am, but he really tips the scale. He's a heavy dude in the truest sense. If you call him Alistair and say it funny, he grabs your feet and yanks them out from under you. I made fun of him once. Now I know what it's like to be kissing concrete. From then on I just called him Al. Al shifts his weight from side to side as he walks. Despite his size, he's built like a tank.

If you were to look at us, you'd say we don't look like an alternative band. In fact, Stewy Lyons didn't let us audition when we first asked for a gig at The Dungeon. But tonight was the Battle of the Bands. Any band could enter. Any band could win.

"My hands are sweating," Al said suddenly. "I can't play with sweaty hands."

What's going on? I began to wonder. These two were shedding their tough-guy skins before my eyes.

"You drive, Jeremy," Al said. "I want to just hang my hands out the window and let them dry off."

I didn't know whether to laugh or cry. Thunderbowl was cracking up. We were going to be an absolute flop. Al pulled over to the curb and got out. He came around and opened the door on my side.

"I don't trust Drek driving my van. Last time, he smashed two brake lights. It cost me twenty-five dollars. You drive," he said to me.

I sat for a second without saying anything. "Uh, guys," I began, "I have a confession to make."

Al was shaking his hands in the air. Sweat was literally dripping off. Drek was staring straight into the windshield, his mind fixed on something none of us could see.

"I can't drive," I said. "At least not legally. I haven't got a license."

"Who cares?" Al yelled at me. "Just drive."

So I got out and walked around, sat down in the driver's seat and started the van. I popped the clutch and we lurched out into the traffic. I almost ran over a man walking a pit bull terrier.

"Where'd you learn to drive?" Al grunted.

"I told you, I didn't."

"Maybe you should try shifting," Drek advised in a shaky voice. I was going pretty fast for first gear. The engine was roaring like it was about to explode.

"Oh, yeah," I said. I shifted, grinding my way into second gear without using the clutch. It sounded like I was trying to cut a battleship in half with a chain saw.

"Nice work, Germ," Al criticized, still hanging his hands out to dry.

I decided it was time they knew my real age. I hadn't really lied before. They just assumed I was older. I didn't ever come out and say anything. I just thought we'd never get to play a place like The Dungeon anyway. They served all kinds of booze. I wasn't old enough to drink, so I wasn't old enough to play there. "What I've been meaning to tell you…" I began again.

"Brake," Drek interrupted in a low, uncertain voice.

"Huh?" I asked.

"Brake!" he screamed into the windshield.

"Oops." A stop sign had appeared out of nowhere. It wasn't my fault. I slammed the middle pedal, hoping that it was the right one.

It was. Nearly half a ton of musical hardware slid forward into our backs as we came to a screeching halt. With my nose squished up against the glass I watched a Pepsi truck squeak by in front of us, inches from the bumper. I figured I had done pretty well.

"I'm only sixteen," I announced. "They won't let me play The Dungeon even if we do win."

Whoever won the Battle of the Bands was going to get a contract to play four nights a week. The money was good and The Dungeon had the wildest audience in town. But now my little secret was out. And now the dream might not come true. Not for me. Not for any of us.

Drek gave me a look of despair. Al just glared at me from across the van. He was rubbing a bump on his head where a flying mike stand had connected with the back of his skull.

"Drive," Al said in that low, threatening voice of his. "From now on you're nineteen. And you better play that damn guitar like your life depends on it."

I wasn't in any position to argue with him.

Chapter Two

Cars were parked up and down the street in front of The Dungeon. It was dark, but there were bright lights in the doorway. The smell of stale beer and cigarette smoke was heavy in the air. Inside the bar I could hear a heavy-metal band cranking it out. The battle had begun. I pulled the van to a stop around the corner, half on, half off the sidewalk.

Now I was the one who had the shakes. Drek and Al were calming down. "All we gotta do is stay cool," Drek said.

"Like ice," Al added.

We opened the rusty doors to the van and started to unload. Al dropped his amplifier on his foot and howled like a wounded wolf.

Just then a jacked-up 4x4 pick up truck pulled up behind us. It sounded like the muffler was off. Whoever was driving hopped the curb and drove in tight to the side door of the bar. We were blocked. No way could we get past them to haul our stuff inside.

Already Al was making ugly threats with his fist. Drek was cracking his knuckles and looking very uptight. All I wanted to do was play music. I didn't want any of this.

The driver's door to the truck flew open and Richie Gregg hopped out in a cloud of smoke. I took a whiff and decided it wasn't tobacco.

On the side of the truck was painted The Mongrel Dogs. Now it was beginning to click. The two other Dogs, Louie and Ike, rolled out the other side and stood coughing on the sidewalk. Everything they were wearing was black and shredded. The Mongrel Dogs had had a regular gig at the club until their attitude and tendency to fight pushed the owner too far. He decided to hold a Battle of the Bands to find a more reliable act. Richie had heard about us, and I think he thought we were the most likely to beat him out.

"Sweetheart," Richie said, looking at me, "you parked in my space."

"Oh, sorry," I said. I sounded like a total wimp. The Mongrel Dogs began to laugh, as if they had just heard the funniest joke.

Al stepped in. "We were here first."

"Oh," Richie said, "excuse me." He faded back to his truck, reached under the seat and grabbed something. Before we could get a handle on what he was up to, he had a spray can of paint in his hand. He shook it, and then he sprayed something in quick, sloppy strokes on the side of Al's van. *Thunderbowl eats* ... Only he didn't have time to finish. Al grabbed the spray can and heaved it like it was a live hand grenade halfway down the block.

Something bad was about to happen. I wanted to run for cover. But just then the side door to The Dungeon flew open. Stewy Lyons walked out. Stewy is a big, burly guy who looks like a bear with tattoos up and down his arms. He runs the club.

"Who owns this truck?" he asked Richie.

Richie pointed a thumb at himself.

"Park it somewhere else, dinghead."

"Sure," Richie agreed. Too much was at stake for him to do otherwise.

"What about this pile of scrap?" He was looking at the van.

"It's mine," Al answered, deeply insulted.

"Then drive it to a junkyard. Just don't

leave an eyesore like this parked by my place."

"Sure," Al said, defeated. Stewy had stopped the fight—but not for long.

Richie hopped in his truck, gunned the engine and began to back out. He had plenty of room to get by, but he cut the wheel too sharply. The back bumper connected with one of the van's tail lights.

"You idiot!" Al screamed.

"Oh, excuse me," Richie said in a phony voice. He revved the engine again and drove backward halfway up the street, tires squealing the whole way.

Chapter Three

Inside The Dungeon, I felt dizzy. The air in the smoky, crowded room behind the stage smelled like dead skunk.

I was thinking that if I could only get my damn guitar in tune, I might be able to play three chords. I still couldn't breathe right. The band on stage sounded good. But when they finished, nobody clapped. It was a tough crowd. It was going to be a tough night.

The Dogs went on stage before us. It took them forever to get set up and finish their sound check. Richie broke a string and Louie couldn't seem to find the beat on the drums. Ike sounded smooth on bass, but you can't carry an alternative band with just a bass guitar. No wonder Stewy was looking for new talent.

But I had the feeling that tonight was just a matter of luck. The Dogs were having a bad night. I think they smoked too much before going on. Still, Richie had a sort of Mick Jagger bad-boy style that the crowd loved. I kept wondering how they would like me. I had no stage presence at all. All I could do was play a few chords, noodle a few riffs.

When the noise of The Mongrel Dogs finally faded, people stood up and cheered. I thought I heard glass breaking. Even when they were lousy, the Dogs knew how to stir up a place.

Then it was our turn. We had twelve minutes to set up. My guitar still didn't feel right. Al's mike had a bad ground and sounded like a huge mosquito. Drek was popping in plugs and throwing switches like a maniac. And before we were ready, this big light flared up and Stewy jumped up to the microphone.

"You ain't heard these guys before and I ain't heard these guys before. But we're going to hear them now," he said. Real intelligent. Two, maybe three people in the dark corners of The Dungeon clapped. I wanted to chicken out. Backstage, Drek had guzzled several beers. Al had inhaled a few himself, but I was stone straight and shaking in my shoes.

Then Al started tromping a heavy thud on the bass drum. Drek plowed into the keyboard three levels too loud. I was still wondering if I was ready when I felt my fingers start moving of their own accord. All at once we were making music.

In fact, we weren't just making music; we were making mountains of sound. The Dungeon walls threw it back at us like cannon fire. Our amps were set way too loud for the place. I think the crowd was amazed. We looked like three rejects from a church choir. But Thunderbowl came on like an atom bomb.

I was so stunned by the power of the sound that I couldn't do a thing but keep on playing. I tweaked the treble up a notch, cut in the phaser, lowered the reverb and let it cook.

It was one of our own tunes called "Ugly Intruder." No one out there had ever heard it before. I forgot about the crowd. I forgot about the dumb Dogs backstage. There was nothing to think about but me and the band and our avalanche of sound.

We played for ten minutes and drove home every last note. Al sang a barely audible lead and Drek and I tried to do backup vocals, but I don't think our mikes were even on. Toward the end, though, I had a long, crazy riff to play on my guitar. And you know what? It sounded good. It sounded better than I had ever played.

It was like my guitar and my fingers were doing all the work. I just stood there and watched. My fingers danced like fireworks. The lights sent mirror blasts of magic to the four corners of the room. And when I cranked the heat up to the absolute boiling point, we cut the song. Right on cue. Just like in practice.

The audience was stunned by the silence. The place was packed to the rafters and for a moment nobody made a sound. The houselights flicked on and the mob went into hysterics. People kept shouting, "More, more, more."

I looked at Drek. His jaw was hanging down to his knees. Stewy bounded on-stage and grabbed my arm. He shot it up in the air like I had just won a heavyweight fight.

"Whaddya think?" he croaked into the microphone. The tide of human sound swelled. A legend had been born.

Stewy led us backstage like we were long-lost friends. "I think you guys have what it takes," he said to us. Out of the corner of my eye I caught a glimpse of Richie. The guy looked hurt. It was not a look I had expected to see on his face.

"You're all nineteen, right?" Stewy asked.

"Right," Al and Drek said at the same time.

Somebody had put a bottle of beer in my hand. I didn't have a chance to say a thing.

"Because if you're not nineteen," Stewy continued, "you can play here, but you gotta go backstage between sets. No hanging out with the customers or drinking. Otherwise I lose my license."

I should have said something right then. But there was a beer in my hand and this nice-looking girl was giving me the once over. I sure didn't feel like a kid.

"Okay. You got the job. You work Monday through Thursday nights. Set up by eight-thirty. Start at nine. Play three sets and shut down at one. Weekends we bring in big names. And, oh yeah, you start tomorrow." Then he walked away. It wasn't his style to get into long conversations.

"One o'clock in the morning?" I asked Al. I was just starting to get an idea of how complicated my life was about to become.

"What's the matter, Germ? Past your bedtime?" Al grabbed the beer from me and slugged it back.

What the hell had I got myself into? How was I going to make it to school the next day? What would my parents say?

"What if Stewy finds out I'm only sixteen?" I asked.

"Then we're screwed, that's what," Drek said. He leaned over me and made it sound like a threat.

Al grabbed him by the shirt and pushed him back to the wall. "Lay off, buzzbrain. Germ here is the key to our success. This kid has million-dollar fingers. Without him we have no gig. So be nice."

"Okay, okay. I was just goofing. I'm sorry," Drek apologized. I knew he wasn't threatening me anyway.

Just then the girl came up and started talking to me. "I liked your music," she said. "I think you blew them all away." She had long brown hair and a funny crooked smile. She said her name was Suzanne. "Can I buy you a beer?"

I didn't want a beer. I wasn't used to drinking. I wanted to go home. I was tired. But it had been so long since a girl, any girl, had been interested in me that I couldn't just walk away.

"Be a gentleman," Drek urged, pushing a ten-dollar bill into my hand. "Buy the lady a beer."

So I left the guys and sat down at a table and bought her a beer. And then she bought me one. That's how it started. We had this incredibly dumb conversation about different guys she had gone out with. They all sounded like slobs or jerks. She said she had even gone out once with

Richie Gregg. Now she hated his guts. Who didn't?

When I got around to looking at my watch, it said one-fifteen. I was thinking about my parents. I was thinking about the homework I should have finished for tomorrow. I felt a little polluted from the beer. And scared. I'm not sure why. Things were moving too fast.

The music had made me a lot higher than the beer. I didn't want to come down. I looked at Suzanne. I looked around at the crowd thinning out of The Dungeon. And I looked again at my watch. I knew that this whole scene was going to be my downfall.

And I couldn't wait to get started.

Chapter Four

I was still dreaming that I was up on stage when my old man stormed into my bedroom. He walked over to the window and snapped the shade so it flipped up to the top. Sunlight poured in like someone had just turned on a spotlight.

"Jeremy, get up! Where were you last night?" He was walking back and forth in front of me.

"Yeah, well…it's just that…well, the band…we were playing and—"

"Don't start telling me Thunderbolt—"

"Thunderbowl, Dad."

"Whatever. We didn't raise you to be a…a guitar player." His voice was getting louder and louder.

"Dad, you don't understand. Something happens when I'm playing music—"

"Yeah, I'll say something happens. You start forgetting about real life. I should never have bought you that guitar. I'm going to put my foot down. You have to get home at a sensible hour or quit the band."

He was still pacing back and forth, ranting and raving. I stumbled out of bed and picked my clothes up off the floor. I didn't want to hear another word. All I wanted was to get out of there. Forget the socks. I put on my shoes and walked out. So I was a few minutes late for homeroom. You'd have thought I had just set off World War Three.

When I got home for dinner, Dad had cooled down. His company had landed a big fat contract, and as far as he was concerned all was right with the world. He had had his talk with me and now he figured I would do the right thing.

"Well, Jeremy? Have you given some thought to what we talked about this morning?" he said as we sat down around the dinner table.

"Dad, I can't quit the band until they find another guitar player." I was just stalling. No way was I giving up Thunderbowl.

"But you are going to quit?" he asked.

I stared off into space and played with my food.

"We're just worried that you might be getting into some bad habits," my mother said.

"And you are staying out way too late," my father added. "When I was your age, I had to be in bed by ten o'clock."

"Look," I said, "at night is the only time we can get together to practice. Drek and

Al don't get off work until six-thirty. And we've come so far together. You may not believe it, but we are getting really good. I can't let them down now."

There was no way I could tell them the news about our gig at The Dungeon. "But I promise I'll spend more time on my homework. I'll bring my grades up in everything. Even math." I made it sound like I had it all figured out.

My parents looked at each other. Some unspoken message passed between them. "We'll give it a try," my mother said. My dad looked like he had heartburn.

"Great. Thanks." We were just one big happy family again. For now.

I juggled the late nights, the band and school pretty well for the first week. Then the homework and a looming math test got me unglued.

I mean, I never really liked school. I was terrible at math. English was totally boring. French was as much fun as throwing up.

And then there was Modern World Problems. Oh yeah, like we were really going to learn to solve it all. So there I was at midnight, sitting at a table in The Dungeon, hunched over my homework.

"What are you doing?" Suzanne asked.

"Unreal numbers," I answered.

She looked at me like I had just arrived from outer space. "Huh?"

"It's a hobby of mine." I wasn't going to admit I was still in high school.

Suzanne smiled her kind-of-cute, kind-of-goofy smile. "Yeah," she said, "me too."

I had a math test second period and I was trying to figure out what an unreal number was. But it was awful hard with her looking at me like that.

"You really are…different," Suzanne said.

I thought she really meant I was a bit of a nerd. She was hooked on the Germ who played guitar on stage. And she didn't know what to make of the Jeremy who studied unreal numbers.

I really liked Suzanne, even though she was older than I was. And I was flattered that she was coming on to me.

The break was over. As I headed back onto the stage, Suzanne blew me a kiss. I picked up my guitar and threw my math book into my guitar case. Then I flicked on the amp and in a flash we were blasting into "Traction." It was a loud metal song.

"Kick it!" Drek yelled at me above the roar. He meant for me to get a little mean, a little crazy.

So I got a little mean. I got a little crazy. I gritted my teeth and scratched at the strings. I kicked on the flanger pedal and bent the strings to make them cry. The music was all about something very powerful. I didn't know what. But I was good at playing like I was a wild man. Up on stage I could act any way I wanted. And it felt great just to cut loose.

Chapter Five

And then there was Richie Gregg. After the big discussion with my parents, Richie showed up to give me some advice too. I was outside the bar, trying to find the strength to heft my amp into Al's van. Drek and Al were inside wrapping up wires.

"Come here, jerk," I heard a voice from behind me.

I didn't have to turn around to know who it was. Maybe if I blinked he would vanish back into the shadows.

Fat chance of that. A bony hand grabbed my collar and twirled me around. I tried to keep the amp from cracking onto the sidewalk.

Richie pulled me close. He was right in my face and he spat as he talked. "Twerp, you are about to quit your pissy little band," he said. It was some sort of threat. Richie had this crazed look in his eye. I wouldn't have been surprised if he was on something.

I set the amplifier down hard on his foot and he backed off. "You can't make me quit," I told him.

Richie smiled a perfect scumbag smile. "You quit or I'll bust your face."

I was tired, really tired. Everything was such a major hassle. School. My soft-hearted parents. All I wanted to do was go home and go to sleep. Now this.

Richie was baring his teeth, like the

mongrel dog that he was. What could I say to Richie Gregg to get him off my case?

"Man, you can't solve anything with violence," I said out of the blue. I sounded like a saint.

Richie looked at me like I had just spoken to him in Swahili. I picked up the amp and tried to ignore him.

Instead, Richie spun me around and planted a fist in my mouth. It was the first time in my life anyone had ever done that to me.

He knocked out my front tooth, the jerk. It flew to the back of my mouth and down my throat. I choked on it for a second, then swallowed it. All the while I was falling backward into the bumper of the van. But it was like slow motion.

At first there was this satisfied look on Richie's face. Then he seemed kind of worried. Not scared, just worried. He inched away backward as I closed my eyes and tasted the sweet sticky flavor of my own blood.

Al drove me to the hospital because I was covered in blood. The hospital called my parents. My mom and dad arrived and found me minus a front tooth. I told them I had tripped over an extension cord. I am pretty clumsy.

My mother was so upset she could hardly speak. But Dad tore into me on the way home.

"What are you doing with your life?" he asked.

"I had an accident," I answered.

"Yeah, but Jeremy, something is happening to you. I don't like it. You've got to settle down. Look at your face. You're a mess."

"I'm okay," I said.

"Jeremy, it's not just this. I ran into Mr. Langford, your English teacher, and he told me you are on a downhill slide at school. You can't throw your life away. School is too important. And now… now this!"

"Give me a break, Dad!" I said. I really didn't need the hassles.

Somehow it seemed more important than ever that I stay with it. I couldn't let Richie think that he was going to get his way. Besides, I was hooked on the music.

"No," I said. "I'm not quitting."

Chapter Six

Eventually the tooth came out of me the only way it could. Just like the doctor said it would.

My dad sent me to his buddy, Dr. Holgate, who fitted me with a fake tooth that I could pop in and out. When I showed it to Suzanne, she said, "That's really cute. I like it."

Thunderbowl was working on some new tunes. We were really pushing ourselves.

The music had taken over and I loved every minute of it. I was becoming a better guitarist from all the practice and performance. And I kept pushing my limits, trying new things.

But I kept falling asleep in school.

"Try some of these pills," Drek said, pouring some out of a little box into my hand one night.

"No way. I'm not into uppers," I told him.

"Shoot. You buy this stuff over the counter. Not drugs. Just caffeine. Like in coffee."

I hated coffee. But I tried the stuff Drek gave me. It worked for a while, but it wasn't enough. I couldn't find time for fifty pages of reading in Modern World Problems. I had lost my grip on every important verb in the French language. My average in math was a lowly fifty-five, and I just couldn't seem to find the time to get at Langford's term paper, "Alternatives to War."

I didn't fit in at school and I sure didn't fit in at the club. All I really wanted out of life was music and sleep.

Then one day I was sleeping my way through Langford's class. The bell rang and I didn't wake up. Everyone left but me. Langford tapped me on the shoulder.

"Truth time, Jeremy," he said.

I woke up from a dream where I was running away from something. There was a long empty hallway. I don't know what was after me. I was in a daze. I pulled my fake tooth out of my mouth and looked at it. I couldn't remember where it came from.

"Just mellow out for a minute," Langford said.

I yawned. "If I was any more mellow, I'd be dead."

Langford looked unhappy. "Jeremy, what happened to you? It's like someone scooped out your brain and threw it in a ditch. You fall asleep in class. Your grades are in the sewer."

"Mr. Langford, I should tell you, I'm thinking of quitting school." This had been building for a while. It had to be school or music. Not both.

"Why?" he asked.

"You wouldn't understand," I said.

"Try me. I'm all ears."

"It's just something I have to do."

Langford looked upset. He shook his head and didn't say anything else. Then he walked away. I was left alone in a big empty classroom.

That night, driving to The Dungeon with Al and Drek, I told them what I was thinking about school.

"Forget about school," Drek advised me. "You don't need it. You're going to be a legend in your own time."

Drek had hated school and quit. He had always been a failure in school even though he was smart. Drek could read music and electronics magazines twenty hours a day. But school just never clicked.

"Stay in school," Al told me. He acted like a father sometimes. "Summer's coming soon and you won't have no homework to worry about."

"Summer's six months away," I said.

"Well, hang in there."

Great advice.

Chapter Seven

You know, I thought that would do it. Quitting school. Or at least my decision to quit school.

But I kept putting it off. Langford knew and the guys in the band knew that I had decided. I wanted to wait for the right time to tell everyone else. Truth time, like Langford had said.

I decided to tell Suzanne, though. She

always wanted me to talk to her, but I never felt like I had anything to say.

"Suzanne, I've decided to quit school," I said.

"Jeremy, I didn't know you were in college."

"High school. I still go to high school."

Suzanne gave me one of her goofy smiles. "You're not telling the truth."

"No, I'm younger than you. I should have told you. I'm not supposed to be playing here. Or drinking this beer." I took a long hard swallow.

"I bet you're a virgin, too," she said.

"What?"

"Sex," she said. "I bet you haven't had any."

"How would you know?"

"I'm just guessing," she answered. The conversation had turned weird awful quickly. And I wasn't going to own up to the fact that I had never had sex.

"Just because I'm young, it doesn't mean I've led a totally sheltered life," I said, maybe a bit too defensively.

"I believe you," she said. She bit her lip. "And I don't care how old you are. I like you just the way you are."

"Well, I'm glad that's out of the way."

"But I think it's fine you're quitting school. I never felt free until I was out of school."

"You finished?"

"Well, yeah. But I didn't have anything better to do."

The break was over. Time to crawl back into the music. "Just don't tell anyone, please," I said.

"I won't." Suzanne went back to her drink. I went up on stage. Thunderbowl began to wail.

Halfway through the set, I noticed that a guy had sat down with Suzanne. It was Ike from the Dogs. He had ordered a whole table full of beer. I started getting worried.

Then I saw Ike pawing at her. At first she didn't seem to mind. But I did.

Now, Suzanne wasn't exactly my girl-friend. And I was probably just one in a long string of her favorites. That's the way she was. But I didn't trust anyone in The Dungeon. Guys came here to meet girls. Al called the place "the meat market." And Ike was not among my trusted friends.

I saw Suzanne start to push back from him. Ike wouldn't leave her alone.

"Drek, let's take a break now. I need to take care of some business," I said.

"Stewy won't like it," Drek answered.

Al saw what I was worried about and backed me up. "Let Stewy twirl it in his ear." Al announced our break. I unplugged my guitar.

I walked over to Suzanne's table, sat down behind the army of empty beer glasses. Suzanne looked like she'd had enough to drink.

"How are you, Ike?" I asked.

"I was fine until you showed up," Ike answered.

"Sorry to hear that," I said.

Suzanne started to giggle. Ike grabbed her wrist. Now what? I wondered.

She was pulling back from him, but he wasn't letting go. Man, I was getting mad. I knew I was about to get in over my head. I started to count my teeth with my tongue.

"Let go of her, Ike, or you'll be sorry," I said. I was surprised at how convincingly it came out.

"Who's gonna make me?" he snapped. I suddenly noticed how much Ike looked like a caveman.

"We'll give it a try," said a voice from behind him. It was Al, the steamroller. Alongside of him was Drek.

Ike was ready to blow. Al would have had him out cold on the floor in ten seconds. I could have just stood back and watched.

Just then, Stewy walked up. "Everything okay here, boys?"

I smiled. "Yes. Just fine, sir."

"Good, good. I like all my customers to have a good time."

"Well, we were just leaving," Suzanne said in a slurred voice. She grabbed my wrist and pulled me toward the door.

"Where are we going?" I asked.

"We're leaving," she said, fishing her car keys out of her purse.

"Hey, I've got to play another set. Besides, you've had a lot to drink. You shouldn't be driving."

Suzanne gave me a look that could burn through concrete. "Well, I'm leaving. With you or without you." She was wobbling as she walked away. I couldn't let her drive off like that.

I followed her to her red Trans Am and got in. As soon as I sat down, she leaned over and kissed me hard on the mouth. She stuck her tongue halfway down my throat. I thought I'd choke. But I can't say I wanted her to quit.

Just as quickly she pulled away from me. She fired up the car. "Watch this," she said and put the car in reverse, pushing the gas pedal to the floor. We lost a year's worth of good tire tread in thirty seconds as she squealed out of the parking space. Next she jammed the Trans Am into first gear and tore out of there. I was sure we were going to get killed.

"Slow down," I yelled.

"Come on, loosen up," she answered. She was weaving a little and driving way too fast. "Bet you didn't know I was a hotshot driver."

"No, I didn't," I said. "Now cut it out!"

"But you haven't seen anything yet."

We were approaching an intersection. Suzanne downshifted, cranked the wheel hard to the right and threw the car into a screaming full-speed turn.

We almost made the turn, but the Trans Am slid over onto the other side of the road. A car was coming head-on. All I saw were the headlights. Suzanne cranked the wheel hard to the right. Too far. Now we jumped the curb and were speeding across somebody's lawn. Straight ahead was a tree.

Suzanne was pulling hard again on the wheel. But she still had her foot down on the gas. In a panic I reached for the ignition key, yanked it hard and pulled it out.

We were back on the sidewalk now and headed for the street. The car sputtered to a stop.

Suzanne hung her head. I thought she was going to cry. I was too mad to try and be nice to her.

"That was stupid" was all I could say. I was still holding her key chain. The keys felt warm in my hand.

I opened the door and got out.

"Give me my keys back so we can get out of here," she insisted.

"Forget it!" I hollered. I threw them as far as I could off into the dark night.

Then I started walking.

Chapter Eight

I thought I wouldn't want to see Suzanne again. But when she didn't show the next night at The Dungeon, I phoned her house. There was no answer, even though I tried about twenty times.

My playing wasn't so good. I hit some wrong chords in the middle of "Ugly Intruder." At one point I nearly stumbled off the stage.

"What's wrong with you?" Al asked me.

"I don't know," I said. "I guess I don't feel inspired."

"Inspired? Bull. Forget the girl. Get into the music." Al looked over at Drek. "Kids today...I don't know what gets into 'em," he said, shaking his head.

I looked around at the packed house. We had a reputation. We were just about the hottest band in town. Drek said it was time to cut a demo with our own money. We had lots of our own material. But I didn't think we were ready. And I wanted to hold onto some of the money I'd made. I looked out at the crowd again and around at the faces. Something was missing. Suzanne wasn't there.

Then I spotted a familiar face. Langford! My English teacher was here at The Dungeon! He was looking at me. He waved. I pretended I didn't see him.

"Come on, Germ. Stop daydreaming. We have work to play," Drek reminded me.

Al leaned across his drums and whispered, "Get inspired."

So I got inspired. I wanted Langford to know why I was thinking about quitting school. He wasn't such a bad guy. He deserved to know the truth.

I dug deep in my pocket for my favorite guitar pick. I closed my eyes and I let myself climb way inside the music. The old me was back. With my guitar I was off into deep space.

At the end of the set, Langford was standing beside the stage clapping. "We need to talk, Jeremy," he said.

"I don't know if there's anything else I have to say. You can see the whole story."

"Come on," he said. "Just give me a minute."

I could see he was not going to give up that easily. We sat down at a table. The waiter brought us each a beer, but I didn't touch mine. Mr. Langford looked worried. He smiled at me. "That was fantastic music, Jeremy. I can see why you want to quit school. I played bass in a rock band when I was younger. It was 1969. We even opened for the Grateful Dead once."

"No kidding?" I said, forgetting I was talking to my English teacher.

"No kidding," Langford repeated. "But that's ancient history. I just wanted you to know that I know what it feels like. But you should still stay in school. You will have plenty of time for music when you graduate. Don't throw everything away for this."

Now I felt uncomfortable. "Did you come here to hassle me or hear the band play?"

Langford threw his hands up in the air, but kept on talking.

What I didn't know then was that Richie Gregg had been right behind us. He was playing spy and playing dirty. As soon as he began to get the picture he tromped off to get Stewy Lyons.

Richie came back and sat Stewy down at our table. Drek and Al spotted trouble and they came over too.

"Tell Stewy the truth, Germ-brain," Richie said. "You're underage and you're still in school."

Stewy looked really annoyed with the whole scene. Langford and my big mouth could lose us the gig. Al and Drek would be really choked. It would be the end of our having an audience for our music.

"And this guy here is his English teacher," Richie continued. He said "English teacher" like he was talking about some gross disease.

Stewy rolled up his sleeves and flexed his tattoos. He always did that when he was bugged by something. He gave Langford a dirty look. "You got any problems with the kid playing a little music?"

"None at all," Langford answered.

Stewy looked back at Richie.

"He's underage," Richie hissed. "He ain't allowed to play here. He lied to you."

Stewy looked straight at me and shook his head. "You should have told me the truth, kid."

"Yeah," Richie snapped, "and if the city finds out, they're gonna kick him out of here. Maybe they'll even shut you down. Man, you better do something quick."

"Richie," Stewy began slowly, "who's gonna tell the city?"

"Him. Maybe he will," Richie said, pointing at Mr. Langford.

"You gonna report me?" Stewy asked Langford.

Mr. L. just shook his head, no.

"What about you, Richie? Are you gonna tattle on us?"

Richie acted like he was being shoved up against a wall. "Well, I could you know. And that would be the end of Thunderbowl."

Stewy took a deep breath and stood up. He leaned over Richie and breathed heavily into his face. "Richie, if you tell anyone, I promise you I'll fix it so you never get a paying job playing music in this city ever again. Your Mongrel Dogs will be eating out of garbage cans for the rest of your life."

Then Stewy looked at me. "Richie's right about one thing. If you're underage, you're supposed to stay backstage between sets." Stewy's voice was real low, but that was worse than him yelling at me. "If you hang out in the bar, I'm breaking the law. And if I get caught, I get closed down. No kid is getting me closed down." Stewy sounded tough. "From now on, you don't step off the front of the stage, you hear me?"

Suddenly I felt like a little kid being scolded. I nodded. Langford shook his head. Stewy scooped up the beer glasses off the table and walked away.

Richie gave me one final dirty look. "It's not over, Germ-brain. Wait and see."

Chapter Nine

The next day report cards came out. Bad news was written all over mine. Music had ruined my school career.

I walked out the front door of the school, headed for home, not even looking where I was going. Reaching the sidewalk, I almost ran into the side of Al's van parked at the curb.

"Germy," Drek greeted me. "What's wrong with you?" He had on wraparound sunglasses that made him look like an alien. Al was in the driver's seat.

"What are you guys doing here?" I asked. I wasn't going to mention the report card to them. They would just laugh, think it was a hoot.

"We both quit our day jobs," Drek said.

"You what? Why?"

Al laughed. He reached out the window and banged on the roof of the van. He let out a wild war cry and then said, "Get in, let's cruise."

I hauled myself into the back of the van and Al drove off. Something weird was happening. Al was grinning from ear to ear. I had never seen him like this before. "Tell him, Drek," he said.

Drek took off his shades. He squinted at the light. "It's like this, my man. We're about to bust into the big time."

"Yeah, really?" They were putting me on.

"Yeah, really!" Drek said. "Stewy got a call from a scout from one of the record companies. The dude's coming to check us out next week."

"Sounds good, but it might be nothing, you know," I said. I was a real downer.

"Come on, this is our big break, the chance we've been waiting for," Al said, leaning on the horn to move some pedestrians out of the way. "We're good. You've seen how the audience at The Dungeon reacts. Besides, Stewy thinks we've got a shot. He says we're original."

Drek tilted his head back smugly. He was acting like he was the mastermind of the whole thing. "You see, it works like this. If the man likes us, we talk options. The company takes us under its wing, sends us on some backup gigs with bands that have CDs out. We learn the ropes and make a few bucks."

Al cut in, "And if things go well, we get a platinum record and a beach house in Malibu."

"What if the guy doesn't like us?" I asked. "What if we screw it up?"

"So we'll still have the job at The Dungeon. We're making real money. It's time to unload the day work and get on with some serious music." Drek sounded so confident he almost got me believing it. Almost.

When I got home I set my report card down on the table in the kitchen and went up to my room. Later, when I came downstairs to dinner, my parents looked like a death squad. I was about to be lectured to death, the cruelest torture of all.

"Hard day at work?" I asked my old man. My voice was sarcastic. I didn't mean it to be.

"I've had worse," he grunted.

"We've looked at your report card," my mother said, getting down to the nitty-gritty.

"Would you pass the mashed potatoes?" I asked.

My father looked ready to explode.

"Okay. Forget the potatoes," I said. Smart was not the way to play it, but I couldn't help myself.

"Your grades are a disaster, Jeremy. You might not even pass this year. This is terrible," Dad said, staring down at my report card on his plate.

"It could be worse," I said.

"Jeremy, you're not taking this seriously."

"Look, I know what I'm doing," I lied. I tried to make it sound convincing, but my brain was scrambled eggs. I was confused. All I wanted was out of this conversation.

"Tell us then," he said. "What exactly are you doing?"

I took a deep breath. "I'm quitting school to work full-time with Thunderbowl."

I saw tears welling up in my mother's eyes. My father's face was going through all the colors of the rainbow.

"We already have work, Okay? We play four nights a week at The Dungeon."

"That's where you've been going?" he asked. "You've been working in a bar?"

"Yeah. And making good money."

My father was still trying to absorb what I was saying. "You think playing music in a bar is working? Well, let me tell you, you've got some thinking to do!"

"How can they let a kid play music in a bar? He's only sixteen," my mother asked him. She was wiping her eyes with her napkin. Dad ignored her. He was too busy glaring at me.

"You should come and hear us sometime," I said. "We're really good. We won the Battle of the Bands and we're one of the best bands in town."

My father looked flabbergasted. "I am not taking your mother to that place...to that Dungeon."

"But, Dad, be real. Music is really important to me. You bought me my first guitar, remember? Besides, we might be landing a recording contract soon." That was a long shot, but I needed to try and convince him that I was going somewhere, that I couldn't give up.

"Get off it, Jeremy. Record companies don't give contracts to sixteen-year-old kids. You've got to get your feet back on the ground. Your mother and I have let you live in your little dreamworld for too long. You are going to listen to us for once."

Suddenly my old man was the great authority on everything. He thought he could order me around.

"You stay in school and work harder. You quit that stupid band and stay away from those nightclubs before you get into real trouble." Now he had a fork in one hand and a knife in the other, both clenched tightly in his fists. "If you want to stay in this house, you will do as I say. That's final!"

My blood began to boil. So it had come to this. I couldn't believe they could be so unfair.

I got up from the table and walked up to my room. I felt dizzy. It seemed like I had been rocketed through deep space to some other planet. Nothing in the house looked the same. I knew I had to get out of there.

Chapter Ten

I could hear my parents downstairs. They were still talking about my problems at school. Then they got going about how I lied to them, how I couldn't be trusted. Finally I had heard enough. I ran down the stairs and out the front door. Even though The Dungeon was all the way on the other side of town, I started walking in that direction. There was no other place to go.

I made up this fantasy that the record deal came through. Thunderbowl was an overnight success and we became millionaires. I bought my parents a new, fancy house to patch things up. My dad had to admit he was wrong about me and music, and we all lived happily ever after.

But it was just a dream. We might not get a recording contract. I might flunk school. I had come this far, though, and I had to keep going. I had to see it through.

At the first phone booth I came to, I looked up Langford's number and called his house.

"Hi, Jeremy. What's up?"

"Look, Mr. Langford, remember what we talked about the other day? About me and school? Well, I've made my decision. There is more to life than sitting in a boring classroom. I'm quitting. I want you to tell the office for me."

"Jeremy, I think you should consider this more carefully—"

"No, man, I've made up my mind. I'm out of school."

"Look, if it's just your grades, there's still time—"

"It's not just my grades," I told him, my voice cracking. "It's more than that. Come on, I'm just asking you to do this one thing for me."

Langford sounded disappointed. I knew he would be, but he didn't try to talk me out of it. "Well, you'll have to sign some papers. Come by the school in the morning."

"Give me a break. I'm not going to come down there in the morning. Can't you get them to send me the papers?"

There was a stony silence on the line. Then Langford responded. "Where should I have the papers sent?"

I didn't know what to say. My jaw was locked. I felt like somebody was tying a rope around my stomach.

"Jeremy, are you still there?"

"Forget the papers. Just tell them I quit." I slammed the receiver down and walked off toward The Dungeon.

I was almost there when a car turned onto the street and pulled up beside me. When I turned around, I saw that it was Suzanne.

"Hey, mister, do you want a ride?"

I was too tired to say no. I walked to the passenger side and climbed in.

"You saved me from wrecking my car the other night," she said.

"I know," I said.

"Look, I'm sorry about what happened. I have a way of messing up everything. Parents. School. Other guys. Now you."

Traffic was backed up behind us as far as the lights at the intersection. Other drivers were honking at us to move. Suzanne let out the clutch slowly and we began to creep along.

"Hey, if you want to talk about real screwups, you are looking at an expert," I said.

"Not you, Jeremy?" Suzanne gave me a warm smile. I leaned over and kissed her.

"Yeah, me," I said. I told her about everything that had happened in the last twenty-four hours. I told her about storming out of the house and my talk with Langford. Just hearing it out loud made me realize how lost and confused I was.

She gave me a long look. "You know, when this recording scout shows up, I bet he's going to sign you guys up. You're really good. After that, things won't seem so bad."

Her confidence made me feel a bit better. "Are you going to The Dungeon tonight?" I asked her.

"I don't know," Suzanne said. "I was thinking about quitting that scene. I've spent too much time there, wasting my life. I should do something else with my evenings. Maybe I'll go back to school."

"Are you serious?" I said. "Why?"

"Yeah. You've been good for me. Made me realize I could be doing more with my life." She smiled.

"That's great. That's just wonderful," I told her. Honestly, the changes in Suzanne confused me. "But could you just be there tonight? For me?"

"Why?" She looked puzzled.

"I could really use a friend around tonight," I said. "And I think I'll go nuts if I have to sit around backstage by myself."

"Sure. Okay," she said as she pulled up in front of The Dungeon. "I'll see you back here at the end of the first set."

I gave her a quick kiss and climbed out of the car. As she drove off, I began to think that I had missed something about Suzanne before. Because she was older, I had figured she was smarter than me. Now I understood that she was mixed up and struggling to do the right thing, just like me. I was glad she wanted out of The Dungeon. But I knew I didn't want her out of my life.

That night Al and Drek were really wired for sound. They were pretty pumped about quitting their jobs and the prospect of a scout coming to hear us. They had flown away to rock-and-roll heaven, but I was full of doubts. And I couldn't get my act together. I was half a beat off at the beginning of every song.

The crowd could tell we weren't on the money, but something else was wrong as well. Richie and Ike were sitting in the corner, giving us the evil eye.

I tried to concentrate on the music, but I hit a couple of wrong notes.

Richie yelled, "You guys stink!"

Ike took up the cause and shouted, "Throw the bums off the stage!"

Somebody in the crowd told them to shut up, but they didn't. Instead, they stood up and kept on with the insults. Finally, a guy who looked a lot like a biker grabbed Richie from behind. Richie turned and slugged the guy. Then The Dungeon started to go crazy. Other guys were getting into the fight. Girls were screaming. Some idiot started heaving beer glasses around the room.

"Keep playing!" Stewy yelled at us. "Try to calm them down." He and the bouncers were trying to break up the worst of it but not having much luck.

I saw a girl take a spill and get cut pretty bad. Then a glass whizzed past Drek's head and smashed against the wall. He threw what was left of it back into the crowd. It could have hit anyone.

I stopped playing in the middle of the song and went backstage, disgusted.

Suzanne was waiting for me back there. We waited for the noise out front to die down. Only it didn't. I had a quick look out and saw that Al and Drek had waded in and were now part of the brawl. And somewhere out there in the battle were The Mongrel Dogs.

Suzanne suggested we get out of there before the cops came in the front door. I didn't have any better ideas. As the screams got louder, we slid out the stage door and got into her car.

Suzanne drove me to Al's apartment. I had nowhere else to go. We sat out on the back steps and waited for him to show up. At last he came up the sidewalk, and Suzanne got up to go. She gave me a kiss on the forehead.

Al was laughing. "You should have seen what I did to Richie. He never knew what hit him."

"Spare me the details, Al," I said. His shirt was torn and he had dried blood at the corner of his mouth. "You mind if I crash here for the night?" I asked.

"No sweat, Germy." He unlocked the door and let me into a living room that looked like a tornado had struck it. "Pull up a floor and go to sleep."

The cops closed down The Dungeon for two weeks. Stewy was fuming, but he promised we would have the gig back when he reopened. When Drek asked him about the record company scout, Stewy looked blank. Then he said that the guy would probably come by when we were back playing. And then again, maybe not.

That's when things started to go wrong with the band. Maybe it was just me. I couldn't get used to being away from home. We'd practice a couple of hours a day, try out a few new tunes. But my heart wasn't in it. I couldn't feel the music, couldn't get that feeling back.

Now that I was free from hassling parents, I kept waiting for the excitement to begin. But it wasn't easy living with Al's stereo blasting twenty-four hours a day. Sleeping on the couch in Al's apartment wasn't much fun either. The apartment always smelled like a locker room. He was getting on my nerves, and without school or money, life was turning into a major drag. To top it off, I missed stuff from home that I had always taken for granted. Meals, for example. Peanut butter sandwiches were getting pretty boring. But with The Dungeon closed, none of us had any money coming in.

After a couple of days I phoned my parents and told them where I was staying.

Then I told them that I had quit school. But I didn't say anything about The Dungeon closing.

"We want you to come home, Jeremy," my mother said. "Maybe we can come up with some kind of compromise."

"I don't know. Give me some time to figure things out, Okay?" I said. I really wanted to just give in and go home. But I knew if I did that, Thunderbowl was done for and I would have to admit that they were right all along.

"Your dad can get you a job on the inventory counter at his work if you want," my mom told me. "You can try it and see how it goes."

"But I have a job," I said. I meant The Dungeon, but right then I didn't even have that. I had nothing. The whole idea of rock-and-roll stardom was beginning to fade. I still wanted the music. I just didn't know if I wanted all the other hassles that went along with it.

Chapter Eleven

Al and Drek were sure that the Dogs had started the fight at The Dungeon on purpose. They figured that it was the only way they could get the gig back—by making us look bad.

"How do you know?" I asked. It was Friday night after our first week off. We were trying to practice but getting nowhere.

"Logic," Drek said.

"Yeah, right," I said. "What proof do you have? I know they were heckling and being jerks."

"You don't need proof with those Mongrel Dogs. They've been ticked off from the beginning because we took their gig away," Drek answered.

Al picked up the newspaper from what passed for a coffee table. "Hey, guess who's playing the dance at the community center tonight?" he asked. He had a devilish gleam in his eyes.

Drek grabbed the paper from Al's hand. His eyes lit up. "Yeah. Right on. The Mongrel Dogs in person! Maybe we should go check it out."

"Yeah, maybe we should. What do you say, Germ?" said Al.

"Why not?" Practice had been less than inspired. And I kind of wanted to hear what Richie was like as a guitar player. I'd only seen him at the Battle of the Bands, and I don't think he'd had a good night.

But I should have known what Al and Drek had in mind.

The community center was stuffed with high school kids. It felt really weird to be at a scene like this, around people my own age again.

The Mongrel Dogs were tuning up. You could hear them arguing and swearing at each other over their PA system. They seemed pretty crude.

But suddenly Richie held up two fists and they stopped arguing. As he brought his arms down, he hammered a chord on his guitar.

The Mongrel Dogs started playing music. It was louder than any band I ever heard. Louder than Thunderbowl. They came on like a hurricane, and the sound was almost enough to knock you over. At first it just sounded like noise. Angry noise.

But kids were dancing. I kept watching Richie as he slammed away at his poor battered guitar. Very slowly the music moved from raunch to rock. I could actually hear someone singing. There was a backbeat and even a tune to it.

The more I listened, the more I liked it. The crowd was hooting and hollering. They loved it—and I could see why. The Mongrel Dogs had turned all their nastiness into some very fine music.

Not all of Thunderbowl was in agreement with this opinion.

"Listen to that garbage," Al said.

"I think I'm going to puke," Drek said, pretending to heave his guts.

Al pulled us to the back of the hall and into the men's room. The music was still so loud he had to shout.

"I say we get back at them for closing down The Dungeon."

"We don't know they started the fight," I reminded him. "And even if they did, this could make things worse. Just forget it."

"Forget it? Are you crazy?" Drek said.

"Richie tried to get you canned, Germ, remember? We owe him something."

Drek started cracking his knuckles.

"Listen," Al said in a sort of whispered shout. "I have a plan."

I tried to talk them out of it, but it didn't do any good.

When The Mongrel Dogs took their break, we waited until we were sure they were outside, having a smoke. Then, in a flash, we jumped up on the stage.

I felt really strange picking up Richie's guitar and flicking on his amp. I kept asking myself, "What am I doing this for?"

Al sat down at the drums, turned on the microphone. Drek picked up the bass and thumped out a few low mean notes. "We thought you guys might want to hear some real music," Al told the audience.

Al launched into the beat for "I'm Alive." Drek was piecing together a bass riff. My fingers felt like they were frozen. The audience looked puzzled. A few people clapped. But as soon as I saw

The Mongrel Dogs appear at the back door, I wished I had never shown up.

The Dogs were outraged. I watched Richie, Ike and Louie walking through the dancing kids toward us. They were boiling. Behind me, I heard Al give out a maniac laugh. Drek just kept on playing like nothing was about to happen.

I tried to think of an easy way out of this. Nothing was coming but bad news.

So I just stopped playing in the middle of the song.

"Jeremy, you chicken…" Al growled at me through clenched teeth. He was still playing. Then Drek stopped.

I offered Richie back his guitar. Maybe I had chickened out. Or maybe I had realized all along that we were being jerks.

Richie grabbed the neck of his guitar and swung it hard at me like it was a battle-ax. I dodged out of the way just in time and watched it smash into his amplifier. The sound was like an explosion. The guitar busted in half.

Louie had jumped on top of Drek and was trying to choke him. Al had already put a hold on Ike and had him nearly down to the floor. It was getting very ugly.

Several men from the community center started yelling at us. Soon they grabbed us and threw us out into the street.

"If any of you ever show up back here again, we'll have you arrested," one of them said. We had wrecked the dance and we had ruined the gig for The Mongrel Dogs.

But the war was not over. Richie was ready to come at me. His fingers were curled up into claws. There was hate written all over his face.

Al and Drek and the two Dogs were already bashing away at each other again. Some kids had come out to watch and were egging them on.

And I was mad too. But you know, I was angrier at myself than at anyone else. How did I let myself get into this?

"Let's call a truce," I said to Richie.

"Sure," he snarled. "Right after I ruin your face."

I tried to reason with him. "Look, there's no point to this."

"So what?" He swung a lethal fist toward my Adam's apple.

"We shouldn't have messed around with your equipment," I admitted.

"That's right, and now you're going to pay!" Richie threw himself in a headlong dive for my gut. He wanted to bring me down where he could do some real damage.

He charged so fast and so mean that I wasn't about to stand up to him. Instead I dodged out of the way. He lost his balance and fell headfirst into the street.

A car was coming, and the driver slammed on his brakes. The tires screeched as the wheels locked. Richie was right in its path.

I made a lunge to grab him, but instead ran smack into the side of the car. I bounced back to the curb and fell in a heap. The car had stopped. I stood up and looked down at Richie. He was rolling over on his side, his head down under the front license plate. The wheels had come so close to running him over.

Slowly, Richie got to his feet. I saw the fear, the terror in his face.

The driver, a fat man maybe fifty years old, got out and started screaming, "Oh my God! Are you all right?"

Richie was speechless. He shuffled over to the curb and just sat there with his head hung down between his knees.

Al and Drek walked over to me. Their clothes were torn and Drek's glasses were busted.

"I'm quitting," I said. I couldn't take any more of this. I'd just have to learn to live without music.

Richie had the dry heaves. Ike and Louie were trying to calm him down. The driver of the car had gone into hysterics. "The guy just threw himself under my wheels. What was I supposed to do?"

"You can't quit, Germ," Al said. "Not because of them." He pointed at The Mongrel Dogs.

"It's not because of them. It's what's happening to me," I told him.

Chapter Twelve

I went home that night and told my parents what had happened. Nobody gave me a lecture.

"What are you going to do now?" my father asked.

"I'm going to figure something out," I said.

"Can we help?" my mother asked.

"I don't think so. But thanks." It felt good to be home again.

In the morning I phoned Stewy and told him that Thunderbowl needed to meet with him. I said it was urgent. Stewy sounded annoyed, but that was nothing new. I got Al on the line next and told him to get Drek. I wanted them to meet me at The Dungeon in an hour.

Then came the hard part. I had to convince Richie to bring himself and the other Dogs back to The Dungeon.

"Are you out of your mind?" he said on the phone. "You nearly got me killed last night."

"Come on," I said. "Just be there." Then I hung up.

I was sitting on the back steps of The Dungeon when Al and Drek showed up. Richie's pickup pulled in right behind them. You could feel the tension building as everyone got out on the sidewalk.

I didn't give anyone a chance to say a word. "I want to make a deal," I said to Richie. He had a cigarette drooping from the corner of his mouth. I noticed the chain he was wearing for a belt.

"We don't make deals," Louie answered for him.

"What kind of deal?" Richie asked.

"I want The Dogs to share the gig with Thunderbowl when The Dungeon reopens. Two nights a week for you. Two nights for us."

Al grabbed my arm and started to twist. "You've lost your marbles, Germ-brain. We don't make deals with them."

"Then you won't have me on guitar, man. This is the only way I keep playing," I said, loud enough for The Mongrel Dogs to hear.

Al and Drek looked stunned. They waited for me to say something else, but I just kept my mouth shut and let the words sink in.

"We've gotta talk," Drek said, grabbing my other arm and leading me toward the van.

"No," I insisted. "There's nothing to talk about." I pulled away from him and walked over to Richie. "What do you say, Richie?"

"What are we supposed to do in return?" he asked, grinding his cigarette out with his boot.

"Nothing," I told him. "Just play music."

Stewy appeared just then. He looked like he thought he had stumbled into an alligator pit. He couldn't figure out why the alligators weren't fighting. He looked warily around. "What's going on?" he asked.

I explained the arrangement. I told him that everyone had agreed to it. No one said otherwise.

Stewy looked off down the alley at some overflowing trashcans, like he was studying garbage. Then he turned to me. "I like it," he said. "Thunderbowl and Mongrel Dogs, together under one roof. If you can keep from fighting each other, it just might draw some more people. You're on."

Chapter Thirteen

So it's Friday night and Thunderbowl is tuned up and about to begin. But tonight we're not playing The Dungeon. We're playing (can you believe it?) a high school dance. At my high school. And I'm loving every minute of it.

School, in the daytime, is still your basic pain. But when has it been otherwise? I phoned Langford and asked him what I had to do to drop back into school.

"Just start showing up. You've got a lot of work to make up, though." He didn't seem surprised to hear from me.

So I'm back in school. I only play music two nights a week now. It still isn't easy to balance it with the schoolwork, but I'm getting by and I'm not flunking out.

And tonight I get to play in front of all the kids I know. Krista, the cute girl who sits behind me in math class. Alex, who always thought I was a do-nothing dip. Carly, who I grew up with and had a crush on for half my life. Even Gregory Aylesford, who thinks dances need videos instead of bands. They're all here.

Langford is here as a chaperone. I promised him we'd play a couple of old Doors songs and some Grateful Dead. For once, all of these people at school are going to see what makes me tick.

Maybe the best part of it is that Suzanne is here too. It feels sort of funny having her with me tonight. This is such a different world than the bar. But even seeing her standing there, way back in the crowd, I feel like we are good for each other. I know I sound like I have helium in my head, but that's the way I feel.

Drek and Al are still a little ticked off at me, though. We're not making as much money as we did in the old days, for one thing. They both had to get their old day jobs back.

But remember the guy Drek said wanted to come scout us for the record company? Well, he did show up at The Dungeon when we were playing. And he liked us. Next week we get to cut a demo at a studio.

So things are pretty good. I'm getting some more sleep and I can let my guitar cook a couple of nights a week. Too much too soon wasn't such a good idea. And I want to be around to play music for a long time.

What was the line? "Better to burn out than to fade away"? Forget that. I'm not ready for rock star heaven. Besides, tonight is close enough.

So are you ready? I'm going to crank my amp up just a little too high. I give Al the thumbs-up. Now Drek starts to lead us into our opener with a deep, weird synth sound like spaceships taking off or something.

Al kicks in on the bass drum and begins to pound like his life depended on it. In the back of the cafeteria, Langford has cut the lights, all except for a powerful spotlight on us. He points it at me as I hit the first chord. The music roars and drives itself all around the room.

Most of the kids are dancing, but some are just staring at us in disbelief. They've never heard anything quite like this before. Not live anyway.

The sound keeps on growing and it feels like the whole building is going to rise up off the ground. I have this gut feeling that somehow this old school won't ever be the same again.

Blue Moon by Marilyn Halvorson

Bobbie Jo didn't set out to buy a limping blue roan mare—she wanted a colt she could train to barrel race. But the horse is a fighter, just like Bobbie Jo, and that's what made up her mind. Now all she has to do is train the sour old mare that obviously has a past. While she nurses the horse back to health and they get to know each other, Bobbie Jo realizes that the mare, now called Blue Moon, may have more history than she first thought. With the help of the enigmatic Cole McCall, she slowly turns the horse into a barrel racer. Then, when everything seems to be going well, she finds out the truth about Blue Moon and where she came from. Will Bobbie Jo be able to keep the horse? And will she find out why Cole seems to have so many secrets?

Zee's Way by **Kristin Butcher**

And that's when I realized there was someone standing near the end of the wall, watching me. I looked up. My mouth went dry. It was a man with a baseball bat.

Zee and his friends are angry, upset that they are not welcome at a new strip mall and that their old haunt has been replaced by stores that are off-limits to them and by storekeepers who treat them with distrust and disdain.

To get back at the merchants, and to let them know what he and his friends think, Zee paints graffiti on the wall of the hardware store. After the wall is repainted, Zee decides to repeat the vandalism, but this time with more artistic flair. When the store owner catches him in the act, he threatens to call the police—unless Zee agrees to repair the damage.

Orca Soundings

Death Wind by William Bell

Allie's life has just taken a turn for the worse. Not only do her parents fight all the time, but she is failing more classes than not and now she thinks she just might be pregnant. Unable to face up to her parents, she decides to run away. She hooks up with her old friend Razz, a professional skateboarder, and goes on the road. Razz is ranked number one, but constant confrontations with the challenger, Slammer, put Allie in some dangerous situations.

With the rivalry heating up, Razz and Allie head toward home—right into the path of a fierce tornado. To survive in the horror and destruction that follow the storm, Allie has to call on an inner strength she didn't know she had.

Orca Soundings

Sticks and Stones by **Beth Goobie**

No one expected Jujube to fight back when her reputation takes a beating.

Jujube is thrilled when Brent asks her out. She is not so happy when the rumors start flying at school. Pretty soon her name is showing up on bathroom walls, and everyone is snickering and sniping. When her mother gets involved, Jujube's reputation takes another hit. Deciding that someone has to take a stand, Jujube gathers all the other girls who are labeled sluts—and worse—and tries to impress on her fellow students the damage that can be done by assigning a label that reduces a person to an object.

Sticks and Stones is an inspiring—and enlightening—story about standing up for oneself and the importance of self-esteem and respect for others.

Other titles in the
ORCA SOUNDINGS series